TREASURE TRAILS

Kim Blundell and Jenny Tyler

This book contains a series of mazes and maze-type puzzles. You can have fun doing these over and over again, as long as you don't write in the book. Trace the route with your finger, or, for the more difficult puzzles, put a piece of thin, see-through paper over the page and trace the route with a pencil.

Cat's Great Aunt Matilda is a world famous explorer and collector. She has just left to go on one of her treasure hunts, leaving Cat and Mouse in charge of her house. Before she went, she asked them to tidy up for her and baked them one of her very special chocolate cakes as a reward. Cat and Mouse have eaten the cake and are now too full to work. Cat curls up, while Mouse lazily looks around. Suddenly, Mouse shouts, "Come and look at this!" Cat looks up to see Mouse waving a small sack. Cat has to make his way carefully across the attic, as he is so fat and heavy. Can you help him find a way to Mouse? (He can't go anywhere you couldn't.)

Great Aunt Matilda has left her pet spider, Boris, behind. Boris doesn't like Cat and Mouse, but he is curious so he follows them everywhere. Can you find him hiding in every picture?

Inside the sack is a map and a bag of superstrong mints. The map shows part of the town. A label on the map says, "Adventure starts at the tallest tree in the park." Without reading further, Cat rushes to the park. But instead of finding the tallest tree he goes to the shortest one. Can you find Cat and show him the way back to Mouse?

Now help them both find the way to the tallest tree.

Cat and Mouse are in such a hurry, they don't notice that there is a treasure chest in the park and in all the other places they visit from now on. Can you find them all?

They look at the map again. It tells them to go to Uncle Frank's Emporium. It is getting late and Cat and Mouse are hungry. Help them find the route to Uncle Frank's which does NOT pass the front of anywhere they could buy food. Otherwise they won't get there before closing time.

Cat and Mouse rush into Uncle Frank's Emporium. Uncle Frank looks upset. He was looking forward to closing the store and putting his feet up in front of the television. Mouse offers him the superstrong mints and he cheers up. They are a very special brand which Great Aunt Matilda only brings back with her when she has been up Mount Everest.

Uncle Frank gives Cat and Mouse a shopping list each. He tells them they must collect the items in the order they appear on the list. They must then meet at the nearest mirror.

Can you find Mouse's route through the shop? Now find Cat's route.

white floppy hat
rubber boots
striped sweater
blue T. shirt
snorkel
spade
spotted scarf
telescope
First aid kit
flippers
small back pack
green socks

flashlight
short red walking stick
kettle
plate
cup
bobble hat
sun glasses
large back pack
water bottle
pair of gloves
belt
ball (striped)
umbrella

Mouse reaches the mirror first. While he waits for Cat, he notices a scrap of paper with some writing on it. It says, "Find the jacket with rainbow stripes and look in the pockets". Help them find the right jacket.

Mouse found two cheap plane tickets in one of the jacket pockets. Cat found a golden statue of a camel in the other.

When they got to the airport and found their plane, Cat and Mouse could see why the tickets were cheap. The plane was very old and slow. Worse still, it didn't actually land at their destination. They had to parachute to the ground, and landed on the edge of a deep canyon.

All they can see now, in every direction, is desert. After a while, they spot a camel and a camel trader on the other side of the canyon. Help them find the way across the canyon to the camel.

(Don't forget to look for Boris and a treasure chest.)

The camel trader tells Cat and Mouse that they need to go to the nearest town, where their next clue awaits them. He swaps his camel for the golden statue. "Avoid all oases with three trees," he calls as they set off. "The dangerous bandits, Los Trioles, often use these as hideouts."

Can you find the route Cat and Mouse should take to get to the town safely? Los Trioles are hiding somewhere in the picture. Can you find them?

As Cat and Mouse approached the town, the camel reared suddenly and threw them to the ground. When they were able to stand up again, the camel had disappeared.

Now they are scanning the town carefully and eventually spot the camel munching his lunch. Cat and Mouse agree that they would get lost down in the streets. So they decide to work their way along the tops of walls, over roofs and up and down stairs.

Can you help them find their way to the camel?

13

The camel had a parcel hanging from its neck. Inside it, Mouse found a model boat, some keys, 20 caramels and a message saying, "Cross the jungle to the coast by helicopter". After a careful search, they found the helicopter. (Look back over the page to see if you can find it too.)

Cat flew inexpertly over the jungle but Mouse felt ill and made him land in the first clearing they came to.

Now that Mouse feels a bit better, they take off again. But he can only manage the flight from one clearing to the next without feeling sick. Some clearings are not safe to land in. Can you help Cat find a route to the coast along a line of safe clearings?

Cat lands the helicopter on a cliff overlooking a marina. They wonder if their model matches one of the real boats.

"It does!" mumbles Cat, chewing 6 caramels at once. They climb down the cliff and realize they are in a pirate-controlled area. A one-legged man gives them a pirate hat, an eye patch and a parrot, and tells them the rules. At each barrier, they must pay the number of caramels shown on the pink sign. They must not have any caramels left when they reach their boat. Which way should they go?

Cat and Mouse jump on board the boat and wonder
what to do next.

"Ah ha!" exclaims Mouse, as he looks through his
telescope. "There's a signpost on an island over there.
I'm sure it says something about treasure on it." Cat sets
sail. But it is more difficult than he thinks to find the way.
Can you help them find a safe route to the signpost?

As they stared out to sea in the direction of the signpost, Cat and Mouse's hearts sank. They could just make out the tip of an island surrounded by rings of jagged rocks. Just then the parrot squawked, "Pretty Polly! Follow me!"

"I hope she knows where she's going," says Mouse. Can you help Polly find a safe way for Cat and Mouse to sail to the island?

20

Mouse tied the boat up at a derelict jetty. He and Cat are faced with a steep, rocky slope. There are dangers everywhere, including several rare, but deadly cat-and-mouse-eating pumpkins.

They feel sure that treasure awaits them in the ruined temple at the top and are determined to find a way up. Can you help them?

When they reach the temple, Cat spots a carving showing a crown and starts digging around it looking for treasure. Mouse stares at the carving and starts to laugh. "Follow the letters," he chokes. Cat carefully spells out the letters. "After all that!" he sighs.

What does the message on the carving say? Where should Cat and Mouse go now? Go back and help them find the treasure.

Answers

The red lines show the routes through the mazes.

Pages 2-3

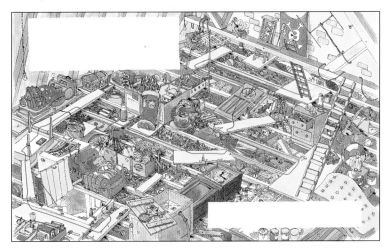

Page 4

Page 5

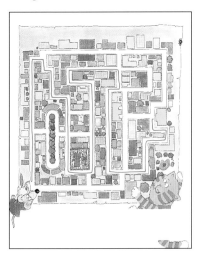

Pages 6-7

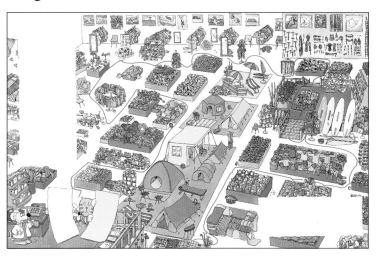

Pages 8-9

Pages 10-11

23

Pages 12-13

Pages 14-15

Pages 16-17

Pages 18-19

Page 20

Page 21

Page 22

To read this, hold the book up to a mirror. The message reads:

You didn't tidy the attic properly did you? Look again and you might find this. (Try the top drawer of the chest on page 3.)